CW00497691

Deadly Murder

by David Foley

A SAMUEL FRENCH ACTING EDITION

FOUNDED 1830

NEW YORK HOLLYWOOD LONDON TORONTO

SAMUELFRENCH.COM

ISBN 978-0-573-69830-9   Printed in U.S.A.   #29305

MUSIC USE NOTE

Licensees are solely responsible for obtaining formal written permission from copyright owners to use copyrighted music in the performance of this play and are strongly cautioned to do so. If no such permission is obtained by the licensee, then the licensee must use only original music that the licensee owns and controls. Licensees are solely responsible and liable for all music clearances and shall indemnify the copyright owners of the play and their licensing agent, Samuel French, Inc., against any costs, expenses, losses and liabilities arising from the use of music by licensees.

IMPORTANT BILLING AND CREDIT REQUIREMENTS

All producers of *DEADLY MURDER* must give credit to the Author of the Play in all programs distributed in connection with performances of the Play, and in all instances in which the title of the Play appears for the purposes of advertising, publicizing or otherwise exploiting the Play and/or a production. The name of the Author *must* appear on a separate line on which no other name appears, immediately following the title and *must* appear in size of type not less than fifty percent of the size of the title type.

DEADLY MURDER was first performed, under the title *If/Then*, at the International Mystery Writers' Festival in Owensboro, Kentucky, on June 14, 2007. It was produced at the Theatre Workshop of Owensboro by Zev Buffman and the RiverPark Center. The performance was directed by Kelley Elder, with sets by Britni Haycox and lighting by Monique Norman. The cast was as follows:

CAMILLE.....................................Jennifer Krahwinkle
BILLY...Claron Hayden
TED. ....Steve Hudgins

DEADLY MURDER was first produced in Europe by Julia Schafranek at Vienna's English Theatre on May 26, 2008. The performance was directed by Julian Woolford, with set design by Simon Scullion, music by Richard John, fight direction by Philip d'Orleans, lighting by Ernst Peinlich, sound by Bruno Gruber, props by Elisabeth Weigel, and wardrobe by Helga Krutzler. The production stage manager was Vernon Marshal. The cast was as follows:

CAMILLE.....................................Amanda Osborne
BILLY ....James Le Feuvre
TED. ....Andrew Loudon

DEADLY MURDER opened at the Devonshire Park Theatre in Eastbourne, under the title *Deadly Game*, on May 28, 2008, preliminary to a UK tour. It was produced by Nick Brooke Limited and Eastbourne Theatres. It was directed by Ian Marr. Design was by Julie Godfrey, with lighting by Douglas Morgan, sound by Clement Rawling, and wardrobe by Judith Rae. The production manager was Paul Debreczeny. The company stage manager was Andrew Jolly. The cast was as follows:

CAMILLE...Karen Drury
BILLY...Kevin Pallister
TED. ....Steven Pinder

DEADLY MURDER opened at the Mill at Sonning Eye on April 23, 2009. Artistic Director, Sally Hughes. It was directed by David Taylor, with set design by Terry Parsons, lighting by Matthew Bliss, music by Glyn Kerslake, fight direction by Alison de Burgh, and wardrobe by Jane Kidd. The cast was as follows:

CAMILLE...Rula Lenska
BILLY...Steven Clarke
TED. ....Tony O'Callaghan

CHARACTERS

CAMILLE

BILLY

TED

SETTING

Manhattan. The living room of a converted Soho loft. The room is furnished in what might be called High Soho Modern with a preference for distressed surfaces, exposed pipes, and dark metallic shades. The walls are painted a textured bronze.

Center right, a doorway leads to a vestibule and the elevator. Just above it, part of the kitchen can be seen. A breakfast bar sheathed in beaten copper thrusts into the room with a couple of tall stools in front of it.

Left of the kitchen, a hallway leads to the guest bedroom, bathroom, and other rooms. Another doorway, up left, swagged in heavy olive drapes, leads to the master bedroom. Between the two doors, up center, is a steel dining table with six chairs placed precisely around it. Above the table is an abstract expressionist painting.

In the left wall, two windows give out on the street, but the drapes are drawn. A small table with a drawer stands between them.

Center stage are a sofa whose sweeping asymmetrical curves are upholstered in copper silk and a couple of dark red armchairs. For the rest there are bookshelves and bibelots, paintings and art photographs, and in the center of the dining table, an ebony and bronze clock in the shape of an elephant.

TIME

The present.

ACT I

(Night. For a moment the room is empty. Perhaps a little music plays softly from somewhere in the apartment. A young man appears from the bedroom up left: handsome, well-built, wearing only a towel. He gazes a moment at the room, taking it in, then starts to move about it, looking at the art, picking up the occasional bibelot, casually, but with a kind of speculative wonder. He has just picked up the elephant clock when CAMILLE *appears in the doorway. She is in her late forties, imperially slim and poised, dressed in a white silk full-length robe. Her hair is cut in a severe pageboy and dyed an uncompromising cherry red.)*

CAMILLE. I wondered where you'd got to.

(He smiles boyishly at her.)

BILLY. You've got a nice place.

CAMILLE. I do. Though I don't necessarily like strange men wandering about it.

BILLY. *(good-naturedly)* Do you think I'm going to steal something?

CAMILLE. One never knows.

BILLY. Well, I'm not going to run out into the streets of Manhattan like this.

CAMILLE. Like Joseph. But that was *without* the towel, wasn't it?

(He looks at her blankly.)

Joseph. From the Bible.

(He gives her another blank look, then smiles.)

BILLY. I wouldn't have taken you for a Bible reader.

CAMILLE. It's a well-known story.

(Pause. He smiles at her.)

BILLY. That was some party, wasn't it?

CAMILLE. I suppose. They get to be a bit of a bore after a while.

BILLY. I guess they must. I bet you go to parties like that all the time.

CAMILLE. As, I'm sure, do you.

BILLY. Sure, but as a waiter.

(She gives him a small smile. He laughs.)

Oh, you were making a joke.

CAMILLE. A little one. Perhaps not a nice one. I'm sorry.

BILLY. *(shrugging)* It doesn't bother me. I won't be a waiter forever.

CAMILLE. You have ambitions?

BILLY. Doesn't everybody?

CAMILLE. Actor? Writer? Painter?

BILLY. I'm not that specific. I just wanna be rich.

CAMILLE. If you want to be rich, you're going to have to get specific.

BILLY. That's good advice.

(He walks around the apartment, appreciatively.)

Did you decorate it yourself?

CAMILLE. More or less.

BILLY. You've got an eye.

CAMILLE. Thank you.

BILLY. I mean it's unusual. Some of these apartments we work at on the Upper East Side – they're all the same. Everything looks really old. Stuffy.

CAMILLE. That's why I don't live on the Upper East Side.

BILLY. How many apartments in this building?

CAMILLE. Just the one.

BILLY. *(astonished)* Really?

CAMILLE. I own the building.

BILLY. *(impressed)* The whole building!

CAMILLE. I bought it back when Soho was cheap.

BILLY. Still…So, what do you do with the rest of the building?

CAMILLE. I've got my studio and offices just below me. And I rent out the shops and storage.

BILLY. Don't you get nervous – a lady living all alone in a big old building?

CAMILLE. I find I like the privacy. I don't like people poking into my business, and in New York somebody always is. *(beat)* Besides, there's a security guard. *(firmly)* Twenty-four hours.

BILLY. That's good. I'd hate to think of you being here all alone.

CAMILLE. That's very kind of you.

BILLY. There are a lot of crazy people in this city.

CAMILLE. Many of them among my intimate acquaintance.

(He gives her a sidelong glance.)

BILLY. That's another joke.

CAMILLE. Yes. Sorry. I'm prone to them.

(He sits on the sofa, smiling up at her with the same boyish good-nature. She glances at her watch.)

BILLY. Camille Dargus…

CAMILLE. *(lightly)* That's my name. Don't wear it out.

BILLY. I think you're famous.

CAMILLE. If you only *think* I'm famous, I'm probably not.

BILLY. What do you do?

CAMILLE. Darling, if we wanted to get to know each other, surely we should have done that *before* we slept together.

BILLY. No, really. What?

CAMILLE. I design jewelry.

BILLY. Really? I had a friend who did that in Portland. It was really great. She sold it every Sunday at the flea market.

CAMILLE. Well, it's a start…

(*He casts another appreciative glance around the room.*)

BILLY. You must've designed a lot of jewelry.

CAMILLE. A fair amount.

BILLY. (*happily*) I knew it! I knew you were famous! You're a famous jewelry designer!

CAMILLE. I have a certain following.

BILLY. I've seen your pictures.

CAMILLE. Well, you've seen more than that now. But now, my dear, I'm afraid it's that time when jewelry designers – even quite famous ones – must get their beauty rest.

BILLY. I bet you don't even design it yourself anymore.

CAMILLE. I design a lot of it. And I have other designers working for me.

BILLY. It's big business.

CAMILLE. It's big business.

BILLY. Wow…

(*pause*)

CAMILLE. Well, now that we've established that I think it's time for bed.

(*He stands, with alacrity.*)

BILLY. Time for bed?

CAMILLE. Time for *me* to go to bed. And time for you to go wherever it is handsome young men disappear to in this big beautiful city.

(*He hesitates, hangs his head.*)

BILLY. Oh.

CAMILLE. I'm sorry. I'm being rude. You'll want to be paid.

(*She reaches for her purse.*)

BILLY. (*sadly*) Naw, I don't want to be paid.

CAMILLE. Don't be silly. It's no problem. And, really, I think for all your trouble –

BILLY. I didn't do it for money.

CAMILLE. Well, that's very sweet. However –

BILLY. Is that what you thought? You thought I was a hustler?

CAMILLE. *(a little embarrassed)* Well, it had crossed my mind, but don't take it personally. Take it as a sign of your –

BILLY. I just thought you were interesting, that's all.

CAMILLE. It's a compliment I wish I could return. As it happens, I only have a weakness for handsome young men in bad tuxes. When they drop a stuffed capon on my plate and whisper would-you-like-more-wine, my heart goes pitter-pat. The problem, of course, is that with waiters one quickly runs out of topics of mutual interest. I believe we've reached that point.

(He hangs his head, sullenly.)

I'm sorry. I'm being unkind. It's just rather late, and I've got a lot to do tomorrow. But I do wish you the best of luck in all your future endeavors. Be happy. Be healthy, wealthy, and wise.

(He doesn't move.)

And, of course, you must let me give you cab fare.

(Still he doesn't move.)

I'll get your things.

(She goes out the upstage door and returns a moment later with his clothes: a waiter's tux, pants, and shoes, and a small gym bag. He accepts them reluctantly from her. Then, changing tack, he opens his towel and does a little bump-and-grind, stripper style, slinging the towel back and forth across his butt.)

Your charms have already been amply noted.

(He closes the towel, slips his tux pants on underneath it, then removes the towel. As he does:)

BILLY. How did you get started in the jewelry business?

CAMILLE. Are you thinking of trying?

BILLY. Just making conversation.

CAMILLE. I guess I had a flair for it.

BILLY. Sure, but how did you get it out there? How'd you get people to notice you?

CAMILLE. I had some seed money. That helped.

BILLY. Investors?

(*beat*)

CAMILLE. The money...came from my husband.

BILLY. Hah! I knew it had to be something like that! Where is he now?

CAMILLE. Dead.

BILLY. I'm sorry.

CAMILLE. Well, life is loss, so they say.

BILLY. Where'd you meet him?

CAMILLE. Do you mind, Billy – it is Billy, isn't it? – I'm not feeling terribly autobiographical tonight.

BILLY. I was just curious. I like to know about people.

CAMILLE. Are you new in town?

BILLY. Pretty new.

CAMILLE. Well, you'll quickly discover that Manhattan is full of people only too willing to share their entire life story on two minutes' acquaintance. And the sooner you get dressed, the sooner you can go seek one out.

BILLY. I'm done now.

(*He makes a show of looking through his gym bag.*)

Is that everything?

(*He slaps his forehead.*)

I almost forgot.

(*He heads for the bedroom.*)

My camera.

CAMILLE. Your – ?

(*He goes off and returns a moment later, holding aloft a small digital movie camera.*)

CAMILLE. Where was that?

BILLY. On your bureau. I put it there when you were in the bathroom. It was pointed at the bed. It's quite a toy. Cost a lot of money, but it's worth it for the picture quality. It takes digital movies. See?

(He plays the movie back, allowing her to look over his shoulder as he does.)

Yup. It's got a real good picture quality. You photograph well. Not many women would look good in that position.

(She reaches for it, but he holds it teasingly up out of her reach.)

Uh-uh.

(She makes a few more swipes for it, then grabs his arm. He pushes her away with a rather too forceful blow to the chest. She staggers back and eyes him warily.)

CAMILLE. What do you intend to do with it?

BILLY. Depends on you. Left to my own devices I might just post it on the web. I've got a website all ready for it. But of course it won't stay there. There'll be thousands of copies all over the world within a few hours. People will be downloading it onto their hard drives. Showing their friends.

CAMILLE. Unless, if I understand your implication, I pay you a large sum of money.

BILLY. Yes.

CAMILLE. Such as…

BILLY. $50,000.

CAMILLE. That *is* a large sum of money, Billy. And nothing I keep lying about the house.

BILLY. You could write me a check.

CAMILLE. What's to keep me from canceling it the minute you leave?

BILLY. If you do, I'll post the video.

CAMILLE. Oh, I see. You're not going to leave me what you've got there.

BILLY. Of course not.

CAMILLE. So how do I know it will be destroyed?

BILLY. You're going to have to trust me on that one.

CAMILLE. I'm beginning to suspect, Billy, that you're not a very trustworthy young man. *(beat)* May I ask you something, Billy? Did you know who I was when we met?

BILLY. Sure.

CAMILLE. You even knew, perhaps, in advance, that I would be at that party tonight.

BILLY. I did my research. I think the key to life is doing your research. I've been watching you. I've seen you at lots of events before this one. You just never noticed me before.

CAMILLE. But you made sure I noticed you tonight. You'd heard – I'm going to make a wild guess here – of certain – well, let's not call them weaknesses – *preferences* of mine.

BILLY. You've got a reputation, if you don't mind my saying so.

CAMILLE. People will talk. And right now you're congratulating yourself on being a very clever boy indeed.

BILLY. Well…

CAMILLE. It worked like a charm.

BILLY. I think so.

CAMILLE. And I fell for it, hook, line, and sinker.

BILLY. I don't like to gloat over a lady's misfortune.

CAMILLE. And you've got me exactly where you want me.

BILLY. Well, don't I?

CAMILLE. I don't think you do, actually. I hate to shatter your little schoolboy dreams, but I do believe there's a flaw in your scheme. Let's say you do post your little *cinema verité*. Let's say you trot home right now and put it up at www.clumsy-attempt-at-blackmail.com for everyone with a hard drive to see. Consider. *What* will they see? They'll see *me* being made love to by a beautiful young man, and *you* sleeping with a woman old enough to be your mother. For which of us will this be humiliating?

(beat)

BILLY. But you're famous.

CAMILLE. And will only be more so if you post your video. As you've doubtless heard before, there's no such thing as bad publicity. And if you think about it – and here the argument gets a little subtle, so pay attention – my jewelry is bought by women of comfortable means who are, like me, a little past the first bloom of youth. Just as car manufacturers want you to believe that if you buy the car you'll get the sexy girl, jewelry designers want women to believe that if you wear their jewels you'll be a magnet for men both adoring and beautiful. What you have in your hand is an unpaid advertisement for Camille Dargus Designs.

(long pause)

BILLY. $20,000.

CAMILLE. I'm afraid not, Billy.

BILLY. 10,000.

(She shakes her head.)

BILLY. 5,000.

CAMILLE. I'm certainly willing to pay you whatever the going rate is these days for boys of easy virtue – if only so you'll leave and I can go to bed – but not a penny more. And you can be sure I know what the going rate is.

(Pause. He puts the camera in his bag, sits on the sofa, and crosses his arms, stubbornly.)

Billy? Did you hear me? The game's up. It's time to go. Oh, for Christ's sake!

(She picks up her purse, takes some money out, and holds it out to him.)

There. That's all you get. Now get up and get out.

(He shakes his head.)

BILLY. I'm not going.

CAMILLE. You're not – ? Of course, you're going. You're either going to stand up right now and go of your own volition, or I'm going to call the security guard and have you thrown out.

(He doesn't move.)

Why? *Why* won't you leave? *(beat)* Your little scheme didn't work. I'm sorry. It was very clever. It really was. I give you credit for your – initiative. I'm sure you'll go far. But, Billy, in this world, and take it from one who knows, when something doesn't work out you've just got to suck it up and move on.

BILLY. Is that what you've done? When something hasn't worked out? Sucked it up and moved on?

CAMILLE. Yes, of course it is.

BILLY. I can't imagine you accepting defeat very easily.

CAMILLE. Sometimes there's no choice. In any case, I'm not going to stand here splitting existential hairs. It's time to say goodnight. Come on, Billy. Milk train's on its way.

(Still he doesn't move. With a sound of impatience, she picks up her cell phone and dials.)

Hello, Ted? I've got an awkward situation up here. A young man who won't leave. Could you – ? Oh, yes, thank you. All right. Thanks.

(She hangs up the phone.)

Ted is on his way up. Very nice man. Very strong man. Beefy. Carries a gun. Been here for years. I give him a nice gratuity every Christmas for just this reason. Because you never know, do you, when a situation like this will arise. Ted will have you out on the cold hard pavement in no time. Or you could save us all some trouble and go on your own steam.

(He doesn't move.)

CAMILLE. *(cont.)* No? Well, suit yourself.

*(They sit silently a moment. **BILLY** sits on the sofa, arms crossed. **CAMILLE** sits in one of the red chairs, picks up a magazine, and starts leafing through it. A buzzer sounds. **CAMILLE** gets up and goes out the stage right door.)*

(off) Hello, Ted. I'm so sorry to disturb you.

TED. *(off)* Don't worry about it. Where's the young man?

*(**TED** enters with **CAMILLE**. He is a man in his thirties dressed in a security guard's uniform.)*

CAMILLE. There he is. Sitting like a lump on my new sofa.

TED. It looks really good there.

CAMILLE. It does, doesn't it? *(to **BILLY**; explanatorily)* Ted helped the boys get it up here last week.

TED. It's an unusual piece.

CAMILLE. One of a kind. My friend Reinaldo designed it specifically for me. To return to the present problem, however, we need to get this young man off it.

TED. Sir, you wanna come with me? *(no response)* Sir, the lady's asking you to go. I believe you've overstayed your welcome.

*(No response. **TED** tugs at **BILLY**'s arm.)*

Come on, sir. Time to go.

*(**BILLY** pulls his arm away.)*

That was the nice way, sir. Do you want me to try the not-so-nice way?

*(**BILLY** doesn't move. With a quick movement, **TED** seizes **BILLY**'s arm again, twists it behind his back, and forces him to his feet.)*

CAMILLE. Oh, good work!

TED. This your bag?

BILLY. *(gasping)* Yes.

*(**TED** picks up the bag.)*

CAMILLE. Oh, I almost forgot. He stole my camera. It's in the bag.

(*TED hands her the bag. She takes the camera out and hands him back the bag. She looks at the camera briefly, then smashes it on the floor. TED stares.*)

It never worked properly.

BILLY. You bitch! That cost a lot of money!

CAMILLE. I know, but what can you do?

TED. Do you want to call the police and have him taken in?

CAMILLE. I'd rather not. They'll just ask a lot of awkward questions, and really what has he done except make a nuisance of himself? Just see that he gets out of the building. Here – (*taking some money from her purse*) – give him cab fare so he knows there are no hard feelings.

(*TED takes the money.*)

TED. All right. This way, sir. Fun's over.

CAMILLE. Good night, Billy.

(*TED starts to force BILLY from the room. Suddenly BILLY hooks his leg under TED's, and TED falls crashing to the ground. BILLY throws himself on top of him and snatches his gun from his holster. He leaps backward, pointing the gun at TED. TED staggers to his feet, but BILLY whacks him on the head with the gun, and he collapses. BILLY whirls around and points the gun at CAMILLE. Pause.*)

You *are* a clever boy.

BILLY. One thing I know: life is unpredictable so you always gotta have a second plan.

CAMILLE. Never have I felt the full force of that principle till this moment.

BILLY. Give me your belt!

CAMILLE. My belt?

BILLY. From your robe.

(*She hesitates. He shakes the gun at her. She slips the belt out of her robe and tosses it to him. She is wearing a slip*)

*under the robe. He goes to her and ties her hands behind
her back. He drags her over to one of the red chairs and
pushes her down on it. He looks around the room. From
the drapes on the upstage left entrance, he rips free a cord
and ties her feet with it.)*

CAMILLE. This is *not* comfortable.

*(He stands and looks at her with a certain boyish satis-
faction.)*

BILLY. Well, now I guess the tables have turned!

CAMILLE. Your dialogue is developing a certain film noir
quality.

BILLY. I'm just saying. You were pretty sure a minute ago
you had me exactly where you wanted me.

CAMILLE. And now I don't. Oh, fickle fortune! So now that
I'm where *you* want *me*, what is it you want?

(He considers this, almost luxuriously.)

BILLY. I wanna be rich. And famous.

CAMILLE. It's only charity to point out that the path you're
on leads more directly to Riker's Island.

BILLY. Is that so?

CAMILLE. Yes, I'm afraid it is. One doesn't get rich or
famous tying up jewelry designers. There's no market
for it. Even in New York.

BILLY. So tell me, Camille? How does one get rich and
famous? How did you do it? Oh, that's right. You told
me. You married a rich husband. Is that what I should
do? Marry someone rich?

*(He throws himself on his knees in front of her, thrusting
himself between her knees. She draws back.)*

Marry me, Camille!

CAMILLE. I'm sorry, Billy, but in the last few minutes you've
worked your way rather far down my list of potential
spouses.

(He gets up and moves away from her.)

BILLY. Well, don't say I didn't offer.

CAMILLE. The gesture is appreciated.

BILLY. I'll just have to think of something else.

(He looks around him, but then turns with a thought.)

BILLY. You never married again? After your husband died?

CAMILLE. No.

BILLY. Why not?

CAMILLE. I guess I felt once was enough.

BILLY. Didn't like it, huh?

CAMILLE. All marriages have their trials.

BILLY. What was yours? Did he fool around?

CAMILLE. Prodigiously, since you ask.

BILLY. That's just not right. I hate to see someone abuse their marriage vows.

CAMILLE. You're a traditional sort of boy.

BILLY. Well, I was raised traditional.

CAMILLE. Somewhere out in the vast red middle of the country.

BILLY. You could say that.

CAMILLE. Sock hops, soda pop, hayrides.

BILLY. Sounds like you know it well.

CAMILLE. Sunday goin' to meetin'.

BILLY. Didn't everybody?

CAMILLE. Perhaps a few brisk years in reform school on the fly.

(She is stalling for time. She keeps casting anxious, involuntary glances at **TED.** **BILLY** *notices.)*

BILLY. *(cheerfully)* Oh, you don't have to worry about Ted. He's down for the count. I know what I'm doing. And anyway, I've got a gun. I'll just bean him again if he gets up.

CAMILLE. Are you sure he's alive?

(This appears to be a new thought for **BILLY.***)*

BILLY. *(slowly)* Well, I don't rightly...

(He goes over to **TED***, crouches down next to him, peels back one of his eyelids, then the other. He picks up* **TED***'s wrist and feels for a pulse.)*

Uh! There's a little pulse!

(He stands up and grins at **CAMILLE***.)*

I guess I'd better get a move on.

(He looks around the room a moment, then goes to his gym bag and, suddenly business-like, takes out a pair of gloves, and puts them on.)

CAMILLE. Surely it's a little late for that.

(He ignores her and starts to search the room, methodically pulling books off shelves, peering behind them, shaking them open, and putting them back.)

What are you looking for?

(He goes on searching.)

If you tell me what you're looking for, I can tell you where it is. *(No answer.)* Is it money? There's money in my purse. *(No answer.)* And by the bed. In a drawer. In the night table. *(No answer.)* Are you looking for valuables? The place is full of them. Take a painting. Take the silver. Take a pillowcase and fill it up.

(He keeps searching.)

Once again, Billy, I feel you haven't thought this through. What are you going to do? Help yourself to all my things and go running off into the night. As soon as you're gone, I'll call the police. Both Ted and I will be able to give a highly detailed description of you, and you'll be picked up before you've had time to hail a cab. Of course, I'm aware that you now have a gun and that, in theory, you could kill me before you go. You'd have to kill poor Ted as well, but in for a penny, in for a pound. But consider a moment. People may have seen us speak at the party. They may even have seen you come into the building. Besides, everything here is registered. If you try to sell it, it will be traced back to me in a New York second. And then you'll get picked up not just for grand larceny, but double homicide. I think your best bet is to call the whole thing off and find some other desperate socialite to lay your wicked charms on. I assure you, *that* well of opportunity is bottomless.

(He looks at her.)

BILLY. Do you know how a computer works?

CAMILLE. I've been known to operate one.

BILLY. But do you understand the principle behind it?

(She shrugs prettily.)

It's all based on "If this, then what?" All a computer does is make choices based on input. If I do this, the computer does that. If I do something else, the computer does something else. When you program a computer, you teach it how to respond to as many different ifs as possible. The computer breaks down when it runs into an if it doesn't know how to respond to. So a good programmer tries to foresee every possible action on the part of the user and teach the computer how to respond to it.

(beat)

CAMILLE. Well…that was briskly informative.

BILLY. I'm saying that's how you need to live your life. Foresee every possible situation. Every user response. Work out every "if/then" in advance. So don't worry about me. I got it figured out.

CAMILLE. As a life philosophy, it's strangely uncomforting.

BILLY. It's always worked for me.

(He continues his search, then goes off the upstage right entrance. **CAMILLE** *waits a moment, hears* **BILLY** *go into one of the rooms in back. She struggles to her feet, but loses her balance and falls to her knees. She hisses across the room.)*

CAMILLE. Ted! Ted! Oh, for God's sake, Ted!

(She moves towards him on her knees.)

Ted!

(She throws herself up against him, urgently whispering his name. No response. Awkwardly she butts up against him. He moves a little. He opens his eyes and is startled to find her practically on top of him.)

TED. Ms. Dargus...?

CAMILLE. Ted, you've got to get up!

(He struggles unsteadily to his knees, rubbing his head, blinking groggily. She swings around so that he can get at her tied hands.)

Untie me!

(He starts to fiddle ineffectually with the belt, then rubs his head again.)

TED. God. My head's pounding. What happened?

CAMILLE. He hit you.

TED. Who did?

CAMILLE. The boy! *(He squints in befuddlement.)* Ted, you've got to focus. There's a boy here. He's got your gun. He hit you with it.

TED. So that's it. Jesus. My head.

CAMILLE. Yes, I'm sorry.

TED. I could use a Tylenol.

CAMILLE. If ever there was a moment to work through the pain, Ted, this is it! He'll be back any second.

TED. Sorry. Sorry.

*(He turns his attention to her bound wrists, blinking painfully. He can't seem to make out **BILLY**'s knot.)*

Wait a second. No, that's not... What the fuck did he...? Oh. Oh. Aha!

*(**BILLY** appears silently in the doorway up right. He waits a few moments, watching them struggle with the cord. Then:)*

BILLY. *(swinging the gun about insouciantly)* I'm just guessing here, but I'm gonna say that any security guard worth his salt doesn't keep an unloaded gun on him. So I'm gonna say there are bullets in this gun. Which means it can do some serious damage. Which means, as I take it, that you have to do what I say.

TED. It's not a toy. Hold it still.

BILLY. It's OK. I know what I'm doing. I've handled lots of guns in my –

(The gun goes off. **TED** *and* **CAMILLE** *both fall back.* **CAMILLE** *tries desperately to wriggle out of* **BILLY**'s *line of fire.)*

(cheerfully) Shit. Didn't expect that. Now let's see… *(He goes to his gym bag and rifles through it.)* Aha! *(pulling out a pair of handcuffs)* It's amazing what I have in this bag. Call me Mary Poppins.

(He surveys the room. His eye lights on one of the exposed pipes. He goes over to **TED** *and tries to clap the hand-cuffs to his wrist.* **TED** *makes a swipe for the gun.* **BILLY** *presses the gun to* **TED**'s *forehead.)*

Uh-uh. We wouldn't want it to go off again. *(They gaze at each other a moment.)* Hold out your hand.

*(***TED** *holds out his hand and* **BILLY** *closes the cuff on it. Still pointing the gun at* **TED**, *he pulls gently on the other cuff and leads him over to the pipe, locking him to it. With* **TED** *safely immobilized, he turns his attention to* **CAMILLE**.*)*

Now you!

(He springs for her. She shrieks. With one quick move-ment, he throws her over his shoulder and rushes her off into the bedroom. **TED**, *left alone, pulls irritably at the cuffs. A moment later,* **BILLY** *reappears holding* **CAMILLE**'s *bedroom phone aloft, smiling triumphantly. He closes the door after him and plunks the phone down on the table. He sits facing* **TED**.)*

BILLY. *(cont.)* I tied her to the headboard. It's starting to look like a bondage movie in here. *(He stretches indolently.)* I guess I've earned myself a breather. Whew! She's a handful. I don't know how you stand it. I hope she pays you well.

(beat)

TED. You always carry handcuffs in your bag?

BILLY. Well, you never know when they'll come in handy. In fact, it's surprising how often they do. *(TED looks sullenly at him.)* What's the matter?

TED. I don't like handcuffs.

BILLY. Bad memories?

(TED says nothing. They stare at each other a moment. Then, with a theatrical sigh, BILLY stands.)

Oh, all right!

(He places the gun on the table, goes over to TED, and unlocks the cuffs.)

Happy?

(TED throws him an injured look and rubs his wrist.)

TED. You might have warned me.

BILLY. Warned you?

TED. I mean, it wasn't part of the plan.

BILLY. The "plan," Ted? The "plan"? How many times do I have to tell you? There *is* no plan. The plan is what happens. If/then, Ted. If/then.

TED. I just wish I'd known, that's all. *(Pause. He rubs his head.)* You hit me pretty hard there, Billy.

BILLY. I got carried away.

TED. I'm just saying, it hurt.

BILLY. All right. So I'm sorry.

TED. What happens now?

BILLY. Damned if I know. I'm playing it by ear.

TED. Billy...

(**BILLY** *grins boyishly and seizes* **TED***'s shoulders.*)

BILLY. But it's fun, Ted! Remember? It's fun, isn't it?

TED. I guess. I just think we should get what we came for and get out.

BILLY. We will. We will. *(He wanders over to the bedroom door and calls loudly.)* How're you doing in there, Camille? *(A muffled cry.)* I gagged her, too. Can't be too careful. *(briskly)* Well, let's get to work! I'll keep searching in here. You check the back rooms.

TED. This could take all night, Billy.

BILLY. So it takes all night. She's not going anywhere.

TED. Why don't we just ask her?

BILLY. Because she won't tell us.

TED. We could persuade her to.

BILLY. *(distastefully)* It's not a Quentin Tarantino movie, Ted. Anyway, I told you: we can't let her know what we're looking for.

TED. But –

BILLY. Ted, baby. Trust a little. I know what I'm doing.

> (**TED** *starts to say something, then gives up. He goes off up right.* **BILLY** *sits in one of the armchairs for a moment, smiles to himself. Suddenly he jumps up, dashes off up left. In a moment, he returns with* **CAMILLE** *once again over his shoulder. He plops her into an armchair. She glares at him, but she's gagged with a nylon stocking.* **BILLY** *grins at her, then strolls into the kitchen. He returns with a large knife. Casually, he approaches* **CAMILLE***. Her eyes widen in fear. He steps behind her, hovering over her with the knife. She cowers away from him. He is about to slice the gag free, but thinks better of it, sets the knife on the table, and unties it instead.)*

CAMILLE. Jesus…

BILLY. I'm still having fun. Are you?

CAMILLE. Being hauled around like a sack of potatoes isn't as much fun as you'd expect.

BILLY. "A sack of potatoes"? That's a touchingly rustic metaphor, Camille. I bet you're a country girl at heart.

(She stares at him coldly, then notices that **TED** *is gone.)*

CAMILLE. Where's Ted?

BILLY. I disposed of him.

CAMILLE. God!

BILLY. Oh, don't be such a drama queen. I mean he's in the next room. I thought you and me should have some time alone. Quality time. So we could get to know each other better.

CAMILLE. I think I know you quite as much as I want to.

BILLY. If you don't mind my saying so, I think that's a mistaken attitude. It's the things you don't know about a person that trip you up. The more you know, the fewer surprises. Go on. Ask me something.

CAMILLE. What are you looking for?

BILLY. Can't tell you.

CAMILLE. Doesn't that make this a pointless exercise?

BILLY. Well, it's a pointless question. It doesn't have much to do with who I am in my heart of hearts. Don't you want to know the real Billy?

CAMILLE. I –

BILLY. My turn! So your two-timing husband set you up in the jewelry business. *(She says nothing.)* Oh, come on, Camille! Play a little! It'll pass the time. Your husband set you up.

CAMILLE. I didn't say that.

BILLY. You said it was his money.

CAMILLE. He left it to me.

BILLY. Oh, so you started your business *after* he died?

CAMILLE. Yes.

BILLY. I guess you needed something to console you.

CAMILLE. Don't we all.

BILLY. So – I'm just trying to picture it – there you were, alone and widowed in New York… *(He lets it hang. She says nothing.)* You *were* in New York, weren't you?

CAMILLE. No.

BILLY. You came here.

CAMILLE. Yes.

BILLY. After he died.

CAMILLE. Yes.

BILLY. Where did you come from?

CAMILLE. Wisconsin.

BILLY. *(excitedly)* Wisconsin? Really? That's a total co-incidence! *I –*

(**TED** *appears in the doorway up right, holding a wooden box.*)

TED. Billy, I found this. Do you think – ?

(*He stops as he notices* **CAMILLE.** *She gazes at him silently a moment.*)

CAMILLE. Ted… Do you know this young man?

(*He looks sheepishly away.*)

BILLY. Me and Ted are old friends.

CAMILLE. I see. The old double-cross.

BILLY. I told you, Camille, I'm way ahead of you. If/then.

CAMILLE. If/then. But what I don't understand, Billy, is what the program's for. Surely even the simplest program has a purpose. What is it you want?

BILLY. *(to* **TED***; forcefully)* Don't you tell her!

TED. I won't, I won't.

BILLY. Give me that.

(*He takes the box from* **TED** *and sits on the sofa, studying it.*)

TED. Do you want me to…?

(*He indicates the back rooms, wishing to get away from* **CAMILLE**'s *reproving gaze.*)

BILLY. No. Search the kitchen.

(**TED** *obediently goes into the kitchen and starts to search.* **BILLY** *fiddles with the box, trying to see how it opens.*)

CAMILLE. My turn. I suppose Billy's not your real name.

BILLY. Of course not.

(**TED** *stops searching, looks at* **BILLY** *in consternation.*)

TED. It's not your real name?

BILLY. No.

TED. What's your real name?

BILLY. None of your business.

TED. *(hurt)* None of my –

BILLY. Keep looking, Ted. What's *your* real name, Camille?

(*beat*)

CAMILLE. Edna.

(*He looks up from the box.*)

BILLY. Edna?

CAMILLE. Yes. Even for the time, even for the Midwest, it was an eccentric choice. You can hardly blame me for changing it.

TED. Camille's a pretty name.

CAMILLE. Thank you, Ted. I chose it myself.

BILLY. Ted, did you know Camille used to have a rich husband?

TED. Really, Ms. Dargus?

CAMILLE. It's a matter of public record.

BILLY. What happened to him, Camille?

CAMILLE. He –

BILLY. He died, Ted. Isn't that sad? What did he die of, Camille? Was he a lot older than you?

CAMILLE. He was older, certainly.

BILLY. Is that why you married him? 'Cause you knew he'd pop off pretty quick?

CAMILLE. I'm grieved to note, Billy, that you have a somewhat conventional turn of mind.

BILLY. I'm just saying it's convenient. Right, Ted? She marries this rich guy and he –

CAMILLE. *(firmly)* He died, tragically, before his time, mourned by a wide circle of family and friends.

BILLY. Including you?

CAMILLE. Including me.

BILLY. You were devastated?

CAMILLE. I was devastated.

BILLY. But you sucked it up and moved on.

(beat)

CAMILLE. Yes.

BILLY. You're a strong woman, Camille.

(He goes to the table and picks up the knife as if to pry the box open with it.)

CAMILLE. Oh, for God's sake! It's not locked.

BILLY. It's not?

CAMILLE. No. There's a little button. It pops open.

BILLY. Really? Where?

CAMILLE. If you untie my hands, I could show you.

BILLY. Ha-ha. Very funny. *(He finds the button; happily:)* Aha!

(The lid pops up as does a tiny ballerina who twirls slowly to "Falling in Love Again." He examines it carefully for a false bottom but finds nothing.)

(philosophically) Oh, well. *(to TED)* Where did you find this?

TED. The library.

BILLY. I'm going to put it back and look some more. You stay here and keep an eye on her.

(As BILLY passes TED, he gives TED's cheek a lingering caress. Then he's gone. TED looks abashed, avoiding CAMILLE's eyes. He starts ineffectually to search the room.)

CAMILLE. Oh, don't tell me, Ted… You fell for a pretty face.

(He gives her a dark look but says nothing.)

Well, you have my sympathy. I did the same thing. And look where it got me. There's a lesson in there somewhere – for the wise child. Think about it, Ted.

(He doesn't answer.)

CAMILLE. *(cont.)* Wait... Aren't you married?

TED. Uh-huh.

CAMILLE. Children? *(no response)* Two boys, one girl?

TED. It's nice of you to remember.

CAMILLE. So what happened?

TED. I don't know. Billy's got a way about him.

CAMILLE. He seems to have more than one. Where did you meet him?

TED. Over at the Diving Bell. He came in one night while I was having my nightcap. We got to talking.

CAMILLE. And the rest is the stuff of true romance.

(He gives her another dirty look and says nothing.)

Then one day, much to his surprise, he learns that you work in this building. And – what a coincidence! – it's the very building *I* live in.

TED. Something like that.

CAMILLE. But I suspect he knew that already. Don't you, Ted? Don't you think he'd marked you out? Long before he walked into the Diving Bell?

TED. Why would he do that?

CAMILLE. That's a question I can't answer till I know what you're looking for. Are you sure you can't give me one little hint?

TED. He told me not to tell.

CAMILLE. Surely that's odd. What difference could it make?

TED. He said if you knew you'd go wild.

CAMILLE. I'm trussed like a pig. How wild could I go?

(He says nothing.)

CAMILLE. Is it something very valuable? *(no response)* Ted?

TED. Obviously.

CAMILLE. It must be a small thing, the way you're looking for it. I mean, it's not a painting or a statue or – the Maltese Falcon.

TED. Don't you know?

CAMILLE. Honestly I don't.

TED. I think you do. He said you'd deny it.

CAMILLE. That's a pretty safe bet – one way or another.

(Beat. He keeps looking.)

Small and valuable. That means jewels. Is it jewelry, Ted? *(no response)* Well, of course, I have a lot of jewelry. I design the stuff. Most of it's in the jewelry box on my dresser. Locked, of course, but I could give you a key. Or you could smash it open if you're feeling manly. Of course, there are one or two pieces of more imposing value. Those I keep in a safe deposit box at my bank.

TED. Not this one.

CAMILLE. No? Why not?

(He says nothing, continues to search. She watches him.)

Are you going to kill me, Ted? You and Billy? When it's all over? When you've found whatever it is you're looking for? *If* you find it? If it exists?

TED. I hope not.

CAMILLE. Oh, me too. I hope not. But I wonder. You're in it rather deep, aren't you? And so is Billy. What choice will you have?

TED. Billy's got a plan.

CAMILLE. I don't doubt it. The Billys of this world always have a plan. But listen to me, Ted. When the plan doesn't work out, the Billys of this world have a way of landing on their feet. And the Teds usually end up holding the bag. So if it comes down to that, Ted – if it comes down to murder – who do you think is going to be left holding the bag? And what's going to happen to those two little boys and that little girl? When their daddy's up the river for life? You're a nice man, Ted. I know that. You've got a good heart. This is not something you should be doing.

*(**BILLY** has entered on the last few lines.)*

BILLY. Ted's not that nice. He's been in jail. Armed robbery.

CAMILLE. *(astonished)* Really? Is that true?

(**TED** *looks abashed again.*)

How is it possible for a convicted felon to get a job as a security guard?

BILLY. We all lie on our resumes, Camille.

CAMILLE. I'm going to speak to your agency about this.

BILLY. *(to* **TED***)* I'm going to search the bedroom.

(*He goes off upstage left.* **TED** *searches even more uncertainly now.*)

CAMILLE. Ted? I'm afraid I'm going to have to ask you a favor.

TED. What's that?

CAMILLE. This position has become absolutely unendurable. I have a problem with my lower back. If you could even move me to the sofa, it would help a lot.

(*He looks uncertain.*)

Please, Ted? I won't bite.

(*He goes to her and helps her up. She falls against him, seductively.*)

Oops!

(*They stand for a moment like that, her mouth very close to his. Then he picks her up and puts her on the sofa.*)

You'll have to untie my hands as well. *(He hesitates.)* Well, I can't lie flat like this.

(*He shakes his head.*)

Look, Ted. You're two big strong men, and I'm one woman with my feet tied. Plus you have a gun. I'd say the odds are very much in your favor in the event of a struggle. *(beat)* Please? I'm in agony.

(*He unties her hands. She shakes them out and lies back on the sofa.*)

Ohhhh! Thank you! Remind me to give you a raise tomorrow. If you haven't killed me.

(**BILLY** *re-enters. He looks at* **CAMILLE** *lying on the sofa.*)

BILLY. What's she doing there?

TED. She said her back was hurting.

BILLY. So let it hurt. You don't have to be nice to her. Remember what she did to –

(He stops himself.)

CAMILLE. To whom, Billy? What I did to whom?

BILLY. None of your business.

CAMILLE. Is that what this is about? Have I wronged you in some way, Billy? Do I know you?

BILLY. No, Camille. Nothing like that. I've just heard stories, that's all. *(to* **TED***)* I gotta say I'm not making much progress here. I think there's a trick hiding place. Tell us, Camille.

(He jerks her upright on the sofa and puts the gun to her head.)

Where is it? Where's the secret place?

CAMILLE. If you'd just tell me what you're looking for –

BILLY. NO!

TED. Why can't we tell her, Billy?

BILLY. Because we can't.

CAMILLE. This is absurd! I mean it, Billy. I'm losing all patience with this situation.

(As discreetly as possible, she is trying to feel for a place under the sofa.)

BILLY. Tell us or I'll blow your brains out!

CAMILLE. If you blow my brains out, nobody gets anything. Back off, and I'll tell you.

(He pulls away from her.)

You see that painting?

(She points to the painting over the dining table; with the other hand she reaches the spot under the sofa. **BILLY** *moves towards the painting.)*

BILLY. Yes.

CAMILLE. Take it down.

(**BILLY** *takes the painting down.*)

BILLY. There's nothing here.

CAMILLE. *(triumphantly)* All right, boys! Game's up!

BILLY. *(turning)* What?

CAMILLE. Ted, you're a security person. You explain to Billy. It's called a distress button. You press it and, in two shakes of a lamb's tail, the men in blue are at your door.

TED. Distress button?

CAMILLE. All over the place. Including here. Under my beautiful new sofa. Get it, Billy? The police are on their way. If I were you I'd make a hasty –

BILLY. You're lying!

CAMILLE. Ted?

(**TED** *comes over and looks at the underside of the sofa. He pulls free a small electric button.*)

TED. *(appreciatively)* Now that's a beautiful thing...

BILLY. What is it?

(**TED** *gets up abruptly.*)

TED. We gotta go, Billy.

BILLY. What? What is it?

TED. It's like she said. You push the button, the police come. We gotta go.

(**BILLY** *whirls on her.*)

BILLY. YOU BITCH!

(*He shoves the gun up against her temple. She winces fearfully.*)

I'LL KILL YOU!

CAMILLE. *(breathlessly)* If you do, Billy, the police are going to get here and find a dead body and two boys with a lot of explaining to do!

TED. Let's go, Billy!

(**BILLY** *grabs* **CAMILLE**'s *cell phone and shoves it at her.*)

BILLY. Call them! Call them now and tell them not to come!

TED. Billy, I'm telling you! Let's get outta here!

CAMILLE. *(simultaneously)* It doesn't work that way, Billy! Once they get the signal, they have to come!

BILLY. Call them! Tell them you made a mistake!

TED. Billy, no! It's no good! Come on!

BILLY. Call them!

CAMILLE. They have to come! They have to investigate every call! I can't call them off!

TED. She's right, Billy! We have to go!

(**BILLY** *whirls on* **TED**.)

BILLY. NO!

(**TED** *starts backing towards the upstage right entrance.*)

TED. Come on, Billy. This way. There's a fire escape out the back. We have to go *now*!

BILLY. *(brandishing the gun at* **TED**) No one's going anywhere! Not till we get what we came for!

(*With* **BILLY**'s *attention distracted,* **CAMILLE** *tries frantically to untie the cord at her feet.* **BILLY** *shoves the gun up against* **TED**'s *jaw. The next lines tumble over each other.*)

You're not going anywhere!

TED. Don't do this, Billy!

BILLY. We're gonna see this through!

TED. Billy, I'm telling you, I can't go back to jail! I can't do it!

BILLY. We're gonna stay right here, and when they show up, she's gonna tell 'em to go away!

TED. It's not gonna work! Please, Billy! Let's go!

BILLY. Listen to me, you bastard! We're not giving up now!

TED. Billy, please! You don't know what you're talking about!

BILLY. I'll kill you first!

(**CAMILLE** *has loosened the cord. She throws herself from the sofa, stumbling on her numb feet, tripping over the cord, but managing to scramble across the room and grab her cell phone as she goes. At the sound,* **BILLY** *turns to see what she's doing, and in that moment,* **TED** *grabs the kitchen knife from the table and plunges it into* **BILLY.** **BILLY** *gasps.*)

Fuck...

(**CAMILLE** *has just managed to get herself upright against the red chair when she hears* **BILLY**'s *gasp. She freezes a moment, then turns to see* **TED** *pull the knife out of* **BILLY.** **TED** *stands frozen, horrified by what he's done.* **BILLY** *reels away from him and sways a moment, dropping the gun. He staggers towards* **CAMILLE,** *a red stain spreading across his white waiter's shirt.* **CAMILLE** *screams in horror and backs away.* **BILLY** *comes towards her, then stops, sways, and falls at her feet. She screams again and covers her face. Silence. Slowly she takes her hands away from her face and looks up to see* **TED** *pointing the gun at her. Blackout.*)

ACT II

Scene 1

(The lights come up on the tableau that ended the first act. TED trains the gun on CAMILLE. He looks down at BILLY's body, stunned.)

TED. I shouldn't-a done that. Jesus…What the…?

(Thinking quickly, he rushes over to her, wiping finger-prints off the knife handle with his shirttail. He holds the gun to her head and forces the handle of the knife into her hands. She cringes away from him.)

Hold it!

CAMILLE. *(pleading)* Noo…

TED. Hold it! Hold it tight!

(She takes the knife and holds it. Unable to look at it, she squeezes her eyes shut and turns her head away, shaking with revulsion.)

We're in this together, understand?

(She nods tightly, still unable to open her eyes.)

They come through that door, I'm out the back, and you're here with a dead body and a knife with your fingerprints on it. Understand?

(She nods again.)

So what are you gonna do when they show up here?

CAMILLE. *(whispering)* Please! Take it away!

TED. What are you gonna say?

(She drops the knife and staggers away from him, gasp-ing in panic.)

CAMILLE. *(between gasps)* There's no one…coming…

TED. What?

CAMILLE. *(sharply; through waves of nausea)* Think it through, Ted…if there was anyone coming…would I have *told* you they were coming?

(Pause, as this sinks in.)

TED. Jesus…

(She clutches her stomach.)

CAMILLE. Ohh…

TED. What's the matter?

CAMILLE. I can't…stand…blood…

(She puts a hand to her mouth and dashes desperately towards her bedroom, gagging and retching. He follows her and stands at the door.)

TED. I'm watching you!

(After a moment, she comes out, dabbing a damp face-cloth against her face and neck. She looks shaken, but composed. She sits downstage. He gazes at her a moment.)

They're not coming?

CAMILLE. The system's new. It's set up, but not engaged. They had problems – getting it to work.

TED. *(with new respect)* That was some bluff.

CAMILLE. Thank you.

TED. You've got nerves of steel.

CAMILLE. *(indicating the facecloth)* Obviously not.

TED. *(sympathetically)* Scared of blood?

CAMILLE. *(shuddering)* I'm afraid so.

TED. Lotta people are. It's a funny thing, blood.

CAMILLE. Can we not talk about it?

TED. Sure.

(Pause. She dabs at her face.)

CAMILLE. And now, Ted?

TED. Now?

CAMILLE. What do we do now? You've got the gun. I feel you should take the lead.

TED. First we gotta have an understanding, Ms. Dargus.

CAMILLE. Oh, please. Camille. Why stand on ceremony now?

TED. *(a little uncertainly)* All right. Camille. We've got an awkward situation on our hands.

CAMILLE. Nicely understated.

TED. There's a dead body here.

CAMILLE. Yes.

TED. And that's bad for me. I already did time. I don't wanna face a murder rap. Now I got a couple of choices here. Safest thing is to kill you, too. You're the only witness. Dead people don't talk. But I hate to do that. You're a nice lady.

CAMILLE. Thank you, Ted. I appreciate that.

TED. Besides, it's messy. And I like to keep things clean. Second thing I could do is I could walk outta here right now, leave you here with Billy.

CAMILLE. *(shuddering)* Ohhh…

TED. But that's messy, too.

(She nods, weakly.)

CAMILLE. Yes.

TED. It's messy for me, 'cause I'm leaving behind a dead body and a live witness. But if you think about it a minute, I think you'll see that it's messy for you, too. Because it's awkward, right? What are you gonna do? Call the police? They show up. There's you. There's Billy. There's the knife. Take a minute to run that conversation through your head.

CAMILLE. Got it.

TED. It's awkward.

CAMILLE. Difficult.

TED. Sure, you'll tell them I did it, but I'll say I was never up here. Saw the young man go up, but that wasn't so unusual, and I always figured it would get you in trouble someday. You follow me?

CAMILLE. It lacks a certain gallantry, but yes, I follow you.

TED. All I'm trying to point out is you think this is *my* mess, but I can turn it into *your* mess pretty quick. That makes it *our* mess. And we gotta clean it up together.

CAMILLE. All right. *(taking a deep breath)* So how do we do that, Ted?

TED. We gotta get rid of Billy. And we can't take him outta here like that. It's too dangerous. We're never gonna get him outta here in one piece.

(long pause)

CAMILLE. I'm trying desperately not to understand what you mean.

(He picks up the kitchen knife. She puts her hand over her mouth and sways.)

(faintly) There's got to be another way.

TED. Tell me how, Camille.

CAMILLE. You could... wrap him in a blanket. Or something.

TED. There's nothing you can put a body in that it's not gonna *look* like a body. And even this time of night, the streets are full of people. You can't carry a dead body out there. Not a whole one anyway.

CAMILLE. Ted... No...

TED. Maybe I haven't explained this clearly, Camille. It's either this, or I kill you. I'm sorry to be so blunt, but that's just the way it is. *(beat)* Now I'm gonna need some plastic bags.

CAMILLE. *(swallowing hard)* In the kitchen. Under the sink.

(He goes into the kitchen.)

TED. *(from the kitchen)* You got a big suitcase? Nothing too recognizable. Nothing with your initials on it or anything.

CAMILLE. Hall closet.

(He comes out with a box of garbage bags and a large meat cleaver.)

TED. *(pointing up right)* Bathroom that way?

CAMILLE. Second door on your right.

TED. I'm gonna take Billy in there.

> *(He starts to drag BILLY off by the feet, then stops.)*

> Oh, one last thing. I'm sorry to have to do this, but you and I both know that, once I'm down that hall, there's nothing to stop you running like hell and getting the police.

> *(He picks up BILLY's handcuffs and dangles them in front of her. Meekly, she offers her wrist.)*

CAMILLE. I suppose I should be used to it by now.

> *(He handcuffs her to the water pipe.)*

TED. Comfortable? Not too tight?

CAMILLE. Fine.

TED. Remember, Camille. We're in this together. After this, there's no turning back.

> *(He takes BILLY's feet again. Suddenly CAMILLE laughs, an arid, slightly hysterical laugh.)*

TED. What?

CAMILLE. I was just thinking of Billy's "if/then." I guess this is one "if" he didn't allow for.

TED. *(somberly)* I'm not sure I see the humor in it.

CAMILLE. No, of course not. Sorry.

> *(TED drags the body off up right as the lights go down.)*

Scene 2

(A couple of hours later. **CAMILLE** *sits on the floor, still handcuffed to the water pipe. A sound of dragging.* **TED** *appears from upstage right. He heaves a heavy suitcase into the room. His hair is wet and slicked back.)*

TED. I took a shower. When I was done. I figured you wouldn't mind.

CAMILLE. Not at all.

TED. You've got a lot of shampoos.

CAMILLE. It's a weakness.

TED. I think I cleaned up pretty well. You might wanna check just in case. After I'm gone.

(She shudders.)

CAMILLE. I suppose I'll have to. It's not something I can leave for the maid.

TED. It should be OK. I was pretty careful. I know how you feel about…

(He trails off delicately.)

CAMILLE. Blood.

TED. Yes.

CAMILLE. Thank you.

TED. I cleaned these off, too.

(He holds up the knife and the meat cleaver. She nods. He puts them on the table. He comes over her to her and unlocks the handcuffs. She stands and stretches, stiffly.)

CAMILLE. So that's the last of Billy?

(He nods, sadly.)

TED. Yup.

CAMILLE. I don't know about you, but I could use a drink. Anything?

TED. Please.

CAMILLE. What's your poison?

TED. *(hoarsely)* Doesn't matter.

(She goes to the bar and pours them each a healthy shot of scotch. She starts to go over to him, but can't bring herself to go near the suitcase.)

CAMILLE. You'll have to come get it.

(He comes to her and takes the glass. She raises hers. Glumly, he raises his glass and takes a swig. She sits.)

You know, Ted, I've been thinking – well, it's funny the things that run through a girl's head while she's hand-cuffed to a water pipe – and I got to thinking, Why?

TED. Why?

CAMILLE. You're a family man. You've got a wife and kids. Why risk all that by getting involved in this?

TED. I'm a gambler.

CAMILLE. That's apparent from the company you keep.

TED. I mean I've got a problem. I've run up some debts. At the casinos.

CAMILLE. How much?

TED. Enough. Enough so I had to do something. Some-thing to get a lot of money, fast. I got some people on my tail. All I wanna do is pay them off and clear out. Disappear.

CAMILLE. What about your family?

TED. They're better off without me, right? I wanna go somewhere and start all over again. Haven't you ever felt that way? Like you just want to throw it all over and become a new person?

CAMILLE. *(lightly)* I suppose everyone's felt that way at least once in their life. *(beat)* All right. Fair enough. You needed the money. You're a desperate man. And things have turned out for you the way they generally turn out for the desperate. Badly.

TED. I guess so. I never thought it would happen like this.

(He lowers his head.)

CAMILLE. I'm sorry about Billy, Ted. Did you really care for him?

(pause)

TED. I loved Billy. Maybe you think that's funny – *(He darts a look at her. She shrugs.)* But I loved Billy. He was great. He kind of – took you by storm. It was like he had sparks coming off him. And he always had some crazy new idea. If you told him it wouldn't work, he figured out a way it would. And he had a thousand more ideas where that one came from. He just figured everything was possible – if you worked it hard enough. He gave me hope. Maybe that's it. When you're hitting rock bottom, you grab onto anyone who throws you a line. I grabbed onto Billy. I loved the guy. I'd have done anything for him.

(Pause. She studies him.)

CAMILLE. Well…almost.

(He looks at her sharply, then accepts it.)

TED. Almost.

CAMILLE. *(softly)* I'm sorry, Ted.

(He wipes his eyes with his sleeve.)

TED. What can you do, right? Shit happens.

CAMILLE. So it does. *(awkwardly)* Ted…I know that – well, there's no way of saying how difficult that was for you.

TED. Well…it had to be done.

CAMILLE. Life brings us to strange passes sometimes.

TED. Doesn't it.

(pause)

CAMILLE. Well, look. I can't say I'm happy about the events that have gone forward in my little home tonight. But, strange as it sounds, I am grateful you decided not to kill me. You're not going to kill me, are you, Ted?

TED. No.

CAMILLE. Thank you. So I'm going to say we're square. We'll say we fell victim to the same wicked charmer, and maybe you've done us both a favor by disposing of him. I'd rather you hadn't killed him, and when you

had, I'd rather you'd found a less macabre approach
to disposing of the body. But what's done is done. Why
don't we just call it even and call it a night?

(He shakes his head.)

TED. I don't think so, Camille.

CAMILLE. You don't think so?

TED. I mean, I don't think you're gonna get rid of me that
easily. Not after what I just did.

CAMILLE. Now, Ted...

TED. I want what I came for.

CAMILLE. What you came for?

TED. Yes. I want the thing we came for, Billy and me.

(pause)

CAMILLE. The thing you came for?

TED. Yes.

CAMILLE. The mysterious object you were so busily hunting
before things took such an ugly turn?

TED. Yes.

CAMILLE. And now that Billy has gone to the halls of his
ancestors, am I allowed to know what this thing is?

TED. I think you know.

CAMILLE. Do I?

TED. Think, Camille. Something very valuable. Something
people would kill for.

CAMILLE. The clever girl doesn't keep such things about
the house.

TED. This one you have to keep here.

CAMILLE. Why?

TED. 'Cause no one's supposed to know you have it.

CAMILLE. Is it stolen goods?

TED. You could say that.

CAMILLE. So now I'm a fence, is that it? All right, tell me.
What is this valuable, stolen thing I'm so desperate to
keep for myself?

(Pause. He studies her.)

TED. You used to be poor.

CAMILLE. Yes. I was poor.

TED. Billy said.

CAMILLE. Billy did his research. All right. So I was poor. There's no shame in that, Ted. As you know.

TED. Maybe. But I don't think you liked it very much.

CAMILLE. Who does?

TED. But you – you did something about it.

(pause)

CAMILLE. Well, yes, Ted. If you want to know, I was – really – quite shamefully poor. My father died early. Car accident. My mother never should have married him, but life brings you to strange passes – strange hard passes. She raised us by herself. The best she could. Smart woman. For all the good it did her. The world just – ground her down. She looked sixty when she was forty.

TED. Not you, though.

CAMILLE. No. Not me.

TED. Never you.

CAMILLE. Point taken.

TED. So you got married.

CAMILLE. Yes.

TED. Rich man.

CAMILLE. Very rich.

TED. You married him for his money.

CAMILLE. Life is seldom that simple. I married him because he was rich and smart and powerful and would never crack up his car going 80 down a country road because he'd had one too many beers at a roadside bar. I married him because he was exactly the opposite of my whole life up to the point I met him. I married him out of a fierce conviction that I was not where I came from.

(He looks at her mournfully.)

TED. We're all where we come from, Camille.

CAMILLE. At the end of the day, yes, I suppose we are.

TED. Was it a happy marriage?

CAMILLE. It was, not to put too fine a point on it, a brutally *un*happy one.

TED. Yes. Billy said.

CAMILLE. Billy's obsession with my life story seems to have bordered on the pathological. He certainly paid a lot more attention to this old history than I do.

TED. You don't think about it?

CAMILLE. I prefer not to.

TED. Why's that?

(Pause. CAMILLE gets up and moves away from him.)

CAMILLE. There comes a time in the life of even a *very* clever girl when she realizes she hasn't been quite so clever after all. Such a time came for me about six months into my marriage. I suppose, really, it's the familiar story. While I was acquiring my husband, *he* was acquiring *me*. But for what? Not, as it turned out, for anything I thought I brought to the table. Beauty, if you will. Intelligence. Charm. A certain sexual... enthusiasm. No, Gerald was odder than that. Gerald liked to play games.

TED. Games?

CAMILLE. Yes. Games. Little psychological games of stunning subtlety and complexity. Before you knew it, you were in one, and there was no way out except to play it to the end. And the goal of all these games was to undermine your confidence, your courage, your sense of who you were. After two years of marriage, I was a dishrag. I couldn't feel anything anymore. I could barely think.

TED. And you wanted out.

CAMILLE. I wanted out. *(beat)* I sense a plot development.

TED. Early on he gave you something valuable.

CAMILLE. Early on? Before things went bad?

TED. Obviously.

CAMILLE. And this valuable thing – well, traditionally it would be some sort of jewel, wouldn't it?

TED. Sure. On a trip to Jamaica –

CAMILLE. Jamaica. That's a nice touch.

TED. On a trip to Jamaica, you pretended it was stolen.

CAMILLE. The jewel being, of course, heavily insured.

TED. That didn't matter. *He* collected the insurance. You wanted the jewel.

CAMILLE. Why?

TED. Because you wanted out. You wanted to leave him. But there was a catch. You wanted to make sure you'd never be poor again.

CAMILLE. As God is my witness. But, surely, in that case, I would have sold it by now.

TED. You didn't need to. Before you could leave him, he died and left you his money. And, in any case, you're superstitious. You knew what it was like to be poor, and whatever else happened, you always knew you had the jewel. You've kept it, all these years, as your insurance against disaster.

CAMILLE. If I understand the genre of this story correctly, the jewel in question must have a name.

TED. The Emerald Star.

(**CAMILLE** *bursts out laughing.*)

CAMILLE. The Emerald Star? It sounds like a cruise ship! And how much is the Emerald Star supposed to be worth?

TED. Five million dollars.

CAMILLE. Five million dollars?! There's no emerald in the world worth that much money!

TED. It's not just the emerald. It's the setting. Ringed with diamonds and sapphires and set in twenty-four carat gold.

CAMILLE. *(still laughing)* Well, now you *know* the story's a crock! I'd never wear anything that gaudy. Even in my feckless youth. And Billy told you this?

TED. Uh-huh.

CAMILLE. It sounds, Ted, as if your friend Billy had a strain of the Jackie Collins in him.

TED. You're saying it's not true?

CAMILLE. Come on, Ted! Think about it! An unhappy marriage, a stolen jewel of inestimable value, a poor girl determined never to go hungry again.

TED. *(stubbornly)* But you *were* poor. And you said your marriage *was* unhappy.

CAMILLE. Granted. That did not, however, distinguish it from a good many other marriages. And it certainly didn't launch me on a career of crime worthy of a drugstore paperback.

TED. Why would Billy make that up?

CAMILLE. It pains me to say this, Ted, but Billy's relationship with the truth seems at best to have been cordially distant.

TED. I'm saying, why would he go to all this trouble? Why would he come here like this – just for some story he made up?

CAMILLE. Well, then someone sold *him* a bill of goods.

TED. He was smarter than that.

CAMILLE. Even the smartest among us get a little stupid when dollar signs start flashing before our eyes. Perhaps Billy got dazzled by the – *(laughing)* the Legend of the Emerald Star!

TED. I'm not buying it.

CAMILLE. You're not – ? You have to buy it, Ted. I'm sorry, but it's all that's on offer.

TED. No. Billy was sure. He knew what he was talking about.

CAMILLE. Not in this case, I'm afraid.

TED. I think he did.

(Pause. **CAMILLE** *sighs.)*

CAMILLE. Well, we seem to be at an impasse. I can't produce something that doesn't exist, and if you're not going to believe it doesn't, I don't know what else to tell you. What's to be done? We could sit here for an hour or so in embarrassed silence, or you could –

*(***TED*** *takes out the gun and points it at her.)*

TED. Or you could start telling me the truth. Fast.

*(***CAMILLE*** *stands up.)*

CAMILLE. *(with cold dignity)* Now I've had just about enough of this. I won't have any more guns pointed at me tonight, thank you very much. I think I've put up with as much as any girl should have to for one ill-advised pick-up. I've been blackmailed, I've been tied up, and I've had a man I barely know chopped up in my bathtub. And I think I've borne it all with grace and a certain sang-froid – considering the circumstances. But there are limits, Ted. There are limits. No one asked you to come here tonight. No one asked you to stick a knife in your best friend. This is all your own doing and your own choice. We live with our choices, Ted, the best we can. And if you've done it all for nothing, if you've come here chasing an illusion, the proverbial wild goose – well, I'm sorry, but there's nothing I can do about that. I can't produce a fabulous jewel out of thin air just so you can feel your time here has been well-spent. The game is over, Ted. We've played it to the end. It's time for you to go. Taking your luggage with you. Of course.

(Pause. They face each other across the room. Suddenly, he lunges at her and, with the hand holding the gun, slams her across the face.)

TED. YOU'RE LYING!

(She cowers away from him. He forces her up against the wall.)

TELL ME WHERE IT IS!!

CAMILLE. *(frantically)* Ted, you've got to believe me. If I could tell you, I would. There's no such –

TED. WHAT DO YOU THINK I CAME HERE FOR?? FOR *THIS*?? *(He swings his gun towards the suitcase.)* I WANT WHAT I CAME FOR!!

CAMILLE. But you can't have it. It doesn't exist. It –

TED. YES, IT DOES!!

CAMILLE. Christ, Ted! Take what you want! Take money! Take jewels! Strip the place bare! Just –

TED. I want the Emerald Star!

CAMILLE. *Why?*

TED. *Why?* Five million dollars! And I need it! I need it so bad! And the beauty part is, you can't come after me. No one knows you have it. No one can say I took it. That's my safety here. I can walk away free and clear, and no one can say a thing! *It's gonna save me, Camille!* I'm not leaving here without it.

CAMILLE. But if it doesn't exist, Ted. If it simply does not exist –

(He hauls her over to the suitcase, holding the gun to her head.)

TED. You see that, Camille! Take a good look at it! There are only two ways this is gonna end tonight. Either I walk out of here with what I came for and we call it even – I don't touch you and you don't touch me. Or I walk out of here with two suitcases instead of one. You decide! It's your choice, Camille! Your choice!

(She tries to turn her head away from the bag.)

CAMILLE. No, please…

TED. Come on, Camille! Fast! Make up your mind!

CAMILLE. *(weakly)* Don't… please…

TED. Two suitcases! One with Billy! One with Camille! Do you wanna know what it was like – cutting Billy up? I never saw so much blood! I was up to my elbows in it! I thought I'd never get it off me! All that blood! Picture that, Camille! Imagine it's you in that bathtub! If I could do it to Billy, I can do it to you!

(CAMILLE's eyes flutter and her head falls back.)

CAMILLE. Noo….

(She faints. He tries to shake her awake.)

TED. Camille! Camille!

(But she is a dead weight in his arms. He is forced to ease her awkwardly to the ground. As soon as the gun is no longer pressed to her temple, CAMILLE lunges and sinks her teeth into his wrist. Startled, he drops the gun. She pushes at it so that it skitters out of his reach. Frantically, she crawls towards it across the room. He grabs hold of her robe and pulls her back. She kicks herself free, scrambles away from him. She reaches desperately for the gun. Her fingers close on it, and she swings it up and slams it against his head. He draws back just enough so that she can point it at him. For a moment, they freeze like that, CAMILLE on her back, TED on top of her, the gun between them. TED tries to calculate his chances of wresting it from her. He makes a move for it, and she fires past his head. He leaps up and moves several steps backwards.)

Jesus!

(CAMILLE jumps to her feet.)

CAMILLE. That was a practice shot. The next one's going in.

(Pause. He eyes her cautiously.)

TED. You wouldn't dare.

CAMILLE. No?

(She fires another shot past his left side; he flinches.)

TED. *(cannily)* No. I don't think you would. Imagine what happens when that bullet goes in. Blood spurting out of me. I bet it would even get on you.

CAMILLE. That's a risk I'm going to have to take.

TED. Me lying here. Pool of blood getting bigger and bigger.

CAMILLE. *(swallowing hard)* Yes, Ted. I've got the picture.

TED. I don't think you have the nerve.

CAMILLE. Maybe not, Ted. Maybe not. But then, you never know, do you, Ted?

TED. Then the police come, Camille. How you gonna deal with that? Or do you think you can do to me what I did to Billy?

CAMILLE. I haven't gotten where I am today without having to take on a great many difficult and unpleasant tasks.

TED. Is that so?

CAMILLE. It is. However, I don't think anything so drastic will be required. The police will be only too sympathetic. Imagine how terrified I was when I came home to find my trusted security guard rifling through my apartment. I surprised him. He attacked me. I managed to wrest his gun from him. I fired some warning shots, but he kept coming at me. What could I do? The poor man, as will undoubtedly be discovered, had a terrible gambling problem.

TED. And the suitcase?

CAMILLE. What do they care about a suitcase? This is attempted robbery. The suitcase will be neatly stowed away in the guest room, and when I have a free moment, I'll dispose of it wherever it is one disposes of such things. New Jersey, I expect.

TED. Really, Camille? Remember what's in it. Do you really think you can do that?

CAMILLE. As I've said before, I can do whatever I have to. If I have to. But I think it's going to be better for both of us if I don't have to. I think it's going to be better for both of us if we call it a night. Ted picks up the suitcase and bids Camille a fond farewell. Camille goes to bed with a stiff drink and a well-earned sense of accomplishment.

(pause)

TED. You don't dare.

CAMILLE. You could be right, Ted. But then – to put this in terms of risk management – there's a tough downside if you're wrong.

(Pause. He eyes her, calculating.)

TED. All right.

CAMILLE. All right?

TED. All right. You win.

CAMILLE. *(surprised in spite of herself)* I win?

TED. You're a tough lady, Camille.

CAMILLE. It's sweet of you to say so. Now leave. Please.

(He heads for the door.)

Ted? The suitcase.

(He comes back and stands next to the suitcase, gazes sadly at it.)

TED. Poor Billy.

CAMILLE. Poor Billy. Indeed.

TED. It hurt, Camille. It hurt to do that to Billy.

CAMILLE. I know, Ted. I sympathize. I do.

TED. I'm never gonna be able to forget it.

CAMILLE. No more will I. Be that as it may, it's time for you – and Billy – to go. You've both been here – quite long enough.

(He picks up the suitcase and lugs it to the door. He turns before he goes.)

TED. I just wanna say one thing before I go.

CAMILLE. *(impatiently)* Really, Ted. This is hardly the moment for valedictory speeches.

TED. It's not a speech. Just two words.

(Pause. He gazes at her, as if for permission.)

CAMILLE. What?

TED. Mildred Johanssen.

(Dead silence.)

CAMILLE. What?

TED. Just that. Mildred Johanssen.

CAMILLE. I don't understand.

TED. Billy said that when it came right down to it, if you weren't gonna give us the Emerald Star of your own free will –

CAMILLE. That's an odd way to put it.

TED. – if you weren't gonna *cooperate* – all we had to say was those two words. Mildred Johanssen.

CAMILLE. And who is Mildred Johanssen?

TED. Billy said you'd know.

CAMILLE. Well, once again, he was wrong. For a boy who prided himself on his research, he seems to have been surprisingly misinformed.

TED. Then why are you so pale?

CAMILLE. What?

TED. You've gone white, Camille. White as a sheet.

CAMILLE. I've been through hell, Ted. Of course I'm pale.

TED. You're shaking.

CAMILLE. All right. Out with it, Ted. Why, at this critical juncture in our lives, do we care about Mildred Johanssen?

TED. Well, for one thing, Mildred was the one that told Billy about the Emerald Star.

CAMILLE. He knew her, then?

TED. Sure he knew her. She was his mother.

CAMILLE. *(sharply)* That's not possible!

(Beat. **TED** *smiles.)*

TED. So you *do* know.

*(***CAMILLE*** lowers the gun, moves into the room, and sits.)*

CAMILLE. All right, Ted. Slay me. Tell me about Mildred Johanssen.

TED. She was a maid.

CAMILLE. A maid?

TED. Your maid. A long time ago. Back in the Midwest. In the house you lived in with your husband.

CAMILLE. And where is Mildred now?

TED. She's dead. She had a hard life after she left you. She drank. She went on welfare. And when she was really scraping bottom, she called up her old boss, and she said, "Ms. Dargus, please help me. I'm at the end of my rope. Give me a job. A handout. Anything." And her old boss said, "Sorry. I can't start giving handouts to any old drunk that calls me up." When Mildred was dying, she told Billy this story. It tore him up. You can imagine. Billy loved his mother, and here she was dying and maybe she wouldn't have died if one very rich woman had put out a hand to help her. It upset Billy.

CAMILLE. Naturally.

TED. It preyed on him. And the funny thing was, Mildred figured you'd be only too happy to help her out, seeing that Mildred once did you an incredibly big favor. She figured you'd remember that.

CAMILLE. Did Mildred say what this big favor was?

TED. Yes.

CAMILLE. And what was it?

TED. You know.

CAMILLE. Do I?

TED. Are you cold, Camille? You're shivering.

(Pause. TED watches her.)

So Mildred told Billy about the Emerald Star. She figured it might come in handy for him. It was information he might be able to use. I guess it was her way of getting some of her own back.

(Pause. CAMILLE shakes her head.)

CAMILLE. (softly) The Emerald Star...

TED. Yes? What about it, Camille?

CAMILLE. *(puzzled)* All of this for the Emerald Star? It doesn't make sense.

TED. Sure it does.

CAMILLE. Does it? *(She studies him carefully a moment.)* It's beautiful, Ted, the Emerald Star. You can't imagine. So clear and lovely. Perfectly cut. It's hard to cut an emerald. You have to be careful. They fracture – so easily. But, if you cut them just right, there's nothing in the world so beautiful. One hundred and twenty carats. Do you know how big that is, Ted?

TED. Pretty big, I'd guess.

CAMILLE. Pretty damn big.

TED. Just give it to me, Camille, and we'll call it quits. No harm done.

CAMILLE. *(a dry laugh)* No harm done… The stone alone is worth close to a million dollars. And the setting – diamonds and sapphires – set in *platinum*, Ted – not gold – yes, I'd say all in all it's worth a cool five million. *(beat)* The first time I looked in the mirror and saw it lying against my neck – I thought, "I've done it. This is it. I've won. I've proved that all you have to do is reach out for what you want and grab it. All it takes is courage and will and smarts." And I was wrong. Well, we know that sad story, don't we, Ted? So one day when we were vacationing in Haiti – not Jamaica – that's another thing Billy got wrong – I paid two local down-on-their-luck types to ransack the hotel room. Told them to take what appealed to them and disappear. The Emerald Star, however, had gone back to Wisconsin in the luggage of my maid – whom family trouble had called away two days previous.

TED. Mildred.

(She looks at him inscrutably a moment.)

CAMILLE. Oh, no, Ted. One more mistake of Billy's. Mildred Johanssen wasn't my maid. She was my sister.

(beat)

TED. Your sister? But – that makes Billy...

CAMILLE. My nephew? No, he wasn't my nephew. Billy was my son.

(Stunned silence. CAMILLE draws a single ragged breath.)

TED. Jesus... But how did he...?

CAMILLE. That's rather a long story, Ted. And we've run out of time for stories. Let's just go about our business. *(She stands.)* Let's get you the Emerald Star and get you out.

(Beat. He is still stunned. She gazes at him.)

CAMILLE. It was supposed to keep me safe, Ted. The Emerald Star. Do you think it will keep *you* safe?

TED. I need it, Camille. I'm sorry. I'm in a bad situation, and I gotta get out.

CAMILLE. All right. So be it.

(She stands, suddenly business-like.)

CAMILLE. You see that little table against the wall?

TED. Between the windows?

CAMILLE. Pull out the drawer.

(He starts to kneel down in front of the table, then turns, suddenly suspicious.)

TED. Put the gun down, Camille.

(She hesitates, then shrugs and lets the gun drop into the chair.)

Stand up against the wall.

(She moves behind the dining table. He kneels in front of the little table. He opens the drawer.)

CAMILLE. All the way out. Put it on the floor.

(He does.)

There's a false back.

(He turns to look at her.)

TED. The Emerald Star?

CAMILLE. The Emerald Star. There's a little catch in the back. It pops open the – secret compartment. *(She laughs suddenly.)*

TED. What's funny?

CAMILLE. Nothing.

TED. I don't see anything.

CAMILLE. It's there. It's small.

TED. It's kind of dark. Do you have a flashlight?

CAMILLE. Oh for God's sake, Ted! Just feel around for it.

(He shoves his hand into the opening and feels around. She moves upstage.)

TED. I'm not getting it.

CAMILLE. Keep trying. It's there.

(He peers into the opening, then sticks his hand in again and feels around. Quietly, she picks up the elephant clock from the dining table.)

CAMILLE. It's over to the right. There. You've almost got it.

TED. I don't feel anything, Camille Are you sure it's not – ?

*(He starts to turn towards her, but she smashes the clock down on his head with all her might. He falls forward, tries to get up. She brings the clock down again. He sinks to the floor. For a moment, she stands there, gasping. She puts the clock down on the floor. Trembling, she stumbles over to the red chair and sits, trying to steady herself, clutching the arms of the chair. She starts to sob. After a moment, she pulls herself together and gets unsteadily to her feet. She forces herself to look at **TED**'s body where it has fallen behind the chairs. Uncertainly, she picks up the clock, looks at it, puts it down. She stands bent over a moment, fighting off a wave of nausea. She picks up her cell phone, starts to dial, then remembers the suitcase. She hangs up and makes herself go over to it. Fighting nausea, she takes hold of the handle. It's very heavy. She starts to drag it backwards, towards the upstage right entrance. **BILLY** appears behind her.)*

BILLY. Need a hand with that?

(**CAMILLE** *spins about, then staggers backwards across the room, screaming. She stops and stares at him in a kind of hopeless astonishment, gasping.*)

It's really heavy. It's full of books. Yours, I'm afraid. We took the liberty.

CAMILLE. What – ? How – ?

BILLY. I told you, Camille. I always have another plan. If/ then.

CAMILLE. But I saw you – I saw him –

BILLY. I really think you're being naïve. It's easy enough to fake a stabbing. They do it in the theatre all the time. You get a knife with a retractable blade. (*He picks up the kitchen knife and demonstrates.*) And the guy getting stabbed wears a packet of stage blood... (*indicating his blood-stained shirt*) It's quite dramatic if you do it right.

(*She looks at him in puzzlement. It's not adding up.*)

CAMILLE. But I saw you get dressed. You didn't have – any such thing.

BILLY. (*with mock exasperation*) Oh, Camille... Think it through. You didn't see me all the time I was here. I planted more than my camera in your bedroom. When I was searching your room, I put the packet on.

CAMILLE. So the fight was – staged.

BILLY. Of course.

CAMILLE. For my benefit.

BILLY. For who else?

CAMILLE. But – you couldn't know – what I was going to do.

BILLY. Now I'm beginning to wonder if you're as smart as everyone says you are. I told you, Camille. I don't have to know what you're going to do. I only have to know what you *might* do. If/then.

CAMILLE. If/then.

BILLY. There were a hundred ways to play this game.

(She stops, stares dully at him a moment.)

CAMILLE. Game?

BILLY. Of course, it pays to do your research. I mean, we knew for instance about the new security system you were having installed. And that it hadn't been hooked up yet. They had some problems setting it up, right? There were some delays?

CAMILLE. Yes.

BILLY. Sure there were. Ted's got a friend in the business. Or he did. *(He looks down at* **TED***'s body.)* Poor old Ted.

CAMILLE. Poor old Ted.

BILLY. So we were ready for you there.

(She sits, looking in front of her with pained puzzlement, as if trying to feel her way through a dense and disorienting fog.)

CAMILLE. But why? What was the reason?

BILLY. I'll tell you what I told Ted. I said, "Ted, it's all about psychology. She's never going to give us that jewel of her own free will. We've got to mess with her mind. So you pretend to kill me and chop me up, and when you've really got her going, I'll come back to life and she'll fall apart. You just say the magic words, and I'll come out."

CAMILLE. The magic words?

BILLY. Mildred Johanssen.

CAMILLE. Mildred Johanssen… But you didn't – come out.

BILLY. And spoil all the fun? My money was on you the whole time, Camille. I knew if it came right down to it, Ted didn't stand a chance. *(She buries her face in her hands.)* Fortunately, I gave him just enough information about Mildred to scare the hell out of you.

(She looks at him.)

CAMILLE. Billy… How much did you know about Mildred?

BILLY. I knew a lot. More than I told Ted. I handled Ted on a need-to-know basis.

CAMILLE. She wasn't my maid, Billy.

BILLY. *(cheerfully)* I know.

CAMILLE. You know?

BILLY. Sure I knew. I knew the whole sad story. Poor Camille – But wait; it was still Edna then, wasn't it? Mildred and Edna. Such plain names for two Midwestern girls… Anyway, poor *Edna* was a wreck. Her horrible husband had just died, and she was pregnant, and she told Mildred, "I'm going to have an abortion." And Mildred said… Come on, Camille. Join in. What did Mildred say?

CAMILLE. *(dully)* "It's a sin to kill a child. I'll take it."

BILLY. And she did. And she named him…?

CAMILLE. William. After our father.

(He nods approvingly at her as at the neat conclusion of a mathematical proof. She looks at him hopelessly.)

CAMILLE. *Why?*

BILLY. *(smiling)* The Emerald Star.

CAMILLE. It doesn't exist, Billy.

BILLY. I know. That was for Ted. Ted loved the Emerald Star. He *believed* in it. Like his last best hope on earth. As it more or less turned out to be.

CAMILLE. But if not for this – fictional jewel – then why?

BILLY. The ancients believed that emeralds allowed you to see the past, present, and future more clearly. They were supposed to improve your memory, too. How's your memory tonight, Camille? *(She doesn't respond.)* You never saw Mildred after you gave her your kid, did you? Why is that, Camille? Why did you never see your own sister again?

CAMILLE. It's what she wanted.

BILLY. That's interesting. Why is that?

CAMILLE. She never called me, Billy. She never asked for help. If you're looking for some kind of revenge or payback –

BILLY. I know she never called you. I just told Ted that. Someone called you all right, but it wasn't Mildred. It was my mother.

(She stares at him.)

CAMILLE. Your mother...?

BILLY. *(with mock impatience)* See, Camille, you're not paying *attention!* I told you my name wasn't Billy. And did you really think I'd come here and sleep with my own mother? What do you take me for?

CAMILLE. *(taking it in)* You're not my son?

BILLY. It's not Greek tragedy, Camille.

CAMILLE. Then who are you?

BILLY. Now that's an interesting story... *(beat)* I bet you knew my mother, Camille. Back when you were Edna. I bet you used to pass her in the hall in high school. But she was one of those things you left behind, like Mildred, on the wrong side of those well-known tracks. You never went back across those tracks, did you, Camille? But Gerald did. He loved to cross those tracks. Anyway, when Gerald died, my mother called up the lawyers and said, "I deserve something here! This is his kid I'm carrying! Goddam it! *Give me some money!*" And do you know what happened?

CAMILLE. There were a lot of women like that. The lawyers took care of them.

BILLY. They did. They paid my mother $50,000 to go away, and she managed to drink and snort it up in less than a year. But it left her kind of bitter. She figured she was owed more than that. She even tried to call you up and threaten you. It galled her to see you walk off with everything. Particularly, since the way she saw it, there had always been something funny about Gerald's death. And she kept saying to me, "Her sister knows all about it. Talk to Mildred." So I did. Poor Mildred... Poor God-fearing, Jesus-loving Mildred Johanssen. It wasn't hard to make friends with Mildred. Her own kid – the other Billy – the *real* Billy – had turned out bad, treating her mean and running off. And she was lonesome. And she felt bad. Like it was all her fault. That was the thing about Mildred. She felt guilty, guilty, guilty. Why did she feel so guilty, Camille?

CAMILLE. Isn't that more or less the point of religion?

BILLY. Maybe. But this was eating away at Mildred. Year after year. And when it had finally eaten right through her – when they'd cut her open and told her there wasn't any hope – I sat by her bed and held her hand, and she made me a very interesting confession. She told me that one night it all became too much for poor Edna – Gerald played one nasty trick too many – and Edna just lost it and smashed his vicious head in. And she got on the phone to Mildred and said, "Come over here quick! I need your help!" And Mildred drove like mad through the Wisconsin night to the really quite impressive spread where Gerald and Edna lived. I went to see it, Camille. It's beautiful. All set in among the pines. Lovely winding paths along the ridge – with some quite startling drops to the river below. And that's where they found Gerald, wasn't it?

CAMILLE. He'd been drinking. We told him not to go out, but he insisted. He wanted to walk the dogs. An hour later the dogs came back and he didn't.

BILLY. That was the story anyway.

CAMILLE. It's the truth.

BILLY. Poor Mildred. She remembered it like someone popped a video into her head. There's Edna. There's Gerald flat out on the floor with his head bashed in. They got him in a wheelbarrow and pushed him out to a likely place along the ridge and dumped him over. Then they walked up and down through the woods, calling his name. And when they'd sufficiently muddied their tracks, they went home, scrubbed the floor, and called the police. Mildred was terrified. They both were. But there was something about Mildred. Everyone knew church-going, God-fearing, hand-to-Jesus Mildred wouldn't lie, and in the end it was *her* they believed. But, as I say, it destroyed her. This terrible sin hanging over her soul – and she couldn't confess to the preacher or a trusted friend or anyone. It's a sad story, isn't it? Mildred and Edna. Two Midwestern girls, looking for a way out. One went for money. One went for God, and it killed her in the end. There's a lesson in there somewhere – for the wise child.

(silence)

CAMILLE. What do you want, Billy?

BILLY. Marry me, Camille.

CAMILLE. Marry you? Why?

BILLY. I told you. I want to be rich and famous. I want to go to parties and travel to glamorous places. I want you to set me up the way Gerald set you up.

CAMILLE. And if I don't want to marry you?

BILLY. I don't think you have a choice. There's Gerald. There's Ted.

CAMILLE. Blackmail.

BILLY. Well...call it a leveraged proposal.

CAMILLE. Billy, why not just come to me? Why not just tell me your story, plain and simple, and then make your "leveraged proposal"?

BILLY. That wouldn't be much fun, would it, Camille? Games are important. Games are how we get to know each other. Games are what bind us together.

CAMILLE. And Ted? Was he part of the game?

BILLY. Oh, I don't think you should feel too bad about Ted. The mob would have got him if you hadn't. He wasn't long for this world, Ted.

CAMILLE. I see. He was...disposable. *(beat)* And if we're going to get married, am I allowed to know your name?

(He smiles slowly.)

BILLY. Gerald.

CAMILLE. Is that true?

BILLY. If it's not, it should be.

CAMILLE. So I'm back where I started...

BILLY. It has a certain pleasing symmetry.

(*pause*)

CAMILLE. I'm sorry about Gerald. I'm sorry about Mildred and your mother and all the rest of it. There isn't a day that's gone by that I haven't thought about that night. All I know is I was trapped. Horribly trapped. I couldn't breathe. And I had to escape. Can you understand that?

BILLY. (*judiciously*) I can certainly *understand* that, Camille. But the sad truth is sometimes you just *can't* escape.

CAMILLE. (*dryly*) Is that tonight's last lesson?

BILLY. For the wise child...

CAMILLE. So be it.

(*With a sigh of resignation, she picks up the elephant clock from the floor.*)

I do feel bad about Ted. What else could I do? He'd backed me into a corner. It's always dangerous... to back someone into a corner.

BILLY. Well, as I said, I don't think you should –

(*Suddenly she hurls the elephant clock at him. He catches it reflexively. She lunges for the gun and points it at him. Freeze.*)

CAMILLE. Put it on the table, Billy.

BILLY. Camille...

CAMILLE. I said put it on the table. (*He does.*) Now back away.

(*He backs away. Blood is on his hands. Still pointing the gun at him, she picks up her cell phone and dials.*)

BILLY. Camille... What are you doing, Camille? Think about this.

CAMILLE. (*into the phone*) Yes. Please. I need help. I've got a terrible situation here. There's a man in my apartment.

He's killed my security guard. I'm holding a gun on him... Yes, it's my security guard's gun... I will. I will... Please hurry, though. I'm not sure how much longer I can hold him like this. *(looking at* **BILLY***)* He may run off into the night – never to be heard from again. Or I may have to shoot him. Just at the moment – it's hard to say...

(She hangs up the phone. The tableau holds for a moment, **CAMILLE** *pointing the gun at* **BILLY***,* **BILLY** *eyeing her warily. The lights go down.)*

The End

FURNITURE & PROPS

ONSTAGE

RIGHT
  Water pipe
  Breakfast bar with two stools
  Partially visible kitchen counters, cabinets.

UP
  Sideboard. On it: Candlesticks, art objects
  Contemporary painting above sideboard
  Dining table with six chairs. On it: bronze elephant clock , cell phone,
  purse with wallet and money
  Swagged drapes with cord ties on bedroom doorway

LEFT
  Bookshelves. On them: books, art objects, photos
  Small table with drawer
  Bookshelves with bar. On bar: bottles, glasses, ice bucket. On shelves:
  more books, photos, etc.

CENTER
  2 Armchairs
  End table. On it: magazine
  Sofa. Under it: electric button
  Coffee table. On it: art books, magazines, ashtray

OFF-LEFT

CAMILLE
  Gym bag. In it: handcuffs, gloves
  Tux, shirt and shoes
  Nylon stocking gag
  Damp facecloth (Act II)

BILLY
  Digital movie camera
  Blood pack
  Land line phone

OFF-RIGHT

BILLY
  Knife with retractable blade

TED
  Gun
  Music box
  Box of garbage bags
  Meat cleaver
  Suitcase

COSTUMES

BILLY
  Towel
  Tux pants
  White shirt
  Bow tie
  Black socks
  Black shoes

CAMILLE
  Full-length silk robe with belt
  Slip
  Watch

TED
  Security guard's uniform, with gun and holster

SET PLAN

WINDOW WITH DRAPES

WINDOW WITH DRAPES

SHELVES

TABLE WITH DRAWER

SHELVES

ARMCHAIR

ARMCHAIR

BEDROOM

END TABLE

DRAPES

SIDEBOARD

DINING TABLE & CHAIRS

SOFA

COFFEE TABLE

HALL

CABINETS

KITCHEN

BREAKFAST BAR WITH STOOLS

WATER PIPE

ENTRANCE